Pirate Patch ★

and the

Treasure Map

In which the fearless
Pirate Patch and his
valiant crew visit the
very scary Skeleton
Island and live to
tell the tale.

For Caydon
R.I.
For Jessica
N.R.

Reading Consultant: Prue Goodwin, Lecturer in Literacy and
Children's Books at the University of Reading

ORCHARD BOOKS
338 Euston Road, London NW1 3BH
Orchard Books Australia
Hachette Children's Books
Level 17/207 Kent Street, Sydney NSW 2000

First published by Orchard Books in 2009

Text © Rose Impey 2009
Illustrations © Nathan Reed 2009

A CIP catalogue record for this book is available from the British Library

ISBN 978 1 84362 978 8 (hardback)
ISBN 978 1 84362 986 3 (paperback)

1 3 5 7 9 10 8 6 4 2
Printed in China

Orchard Books is a division of Hachette Children's Books,
an Hachette Livre UK company.
www.hachettelivre.co.uk

Pirate Patch
and the
Treasure Map

ROSE IMPEY • NATHAN REED

ORCHARD BOOKS

Patch's mum and dad were off sailing *again* in their big, shiny pirate ship – leaving Patch at home.

Towering Turbot!

But they didn't know that Patch
had his own pirate adventures,
with his *valiant* crew: Granny Peg,
Pierre the Parrot, and Portside, his
clever dog.

Jumping Jellyfish!

Their boat wasn't big and shiny,
it was small and a bit leaky.
Patch wanted a new one.
"We need treasure," he growled,
"and lots of it!"

Granny Peg didn't have any
treasure, but she had lots
of treasure *maps*.
Patch grabbed one now.
"Avast, my hearties," he cried.

"Oh no, not Captain Cutthroat's!"
begged Peg. "His treasure's cursed."
But Patch didn't care about curses
and he was the captain.

Let's go!

When they reached Skeleton
Island, a thick cloud of
smoke hung over it.
Even the sand was black.

The others wanted to turn back, but Patch growled, "Drop anchor and prepare to land!"

Everywhere they looked they saw *bad* signs.

Beware!

Haunted Hill

Vale of Tears

FORBIDDEN FOREST

But Patch bravely ignored them and studied the map instead.

You are here. But not for long!

"250 paces due south," he read. Patch set off, taking big strides. Peg, Pierre and Portside followed, fearfully.

They came to another sign
which said:

Tremble All
Who Come Here!

The others trembled,
but Patch bravely went on.

"50 paces due east," said the map.

"50 paces due south."

"50 paces due west."

After 50 paces due north they were right back in the same place. Patch had a feeling that *someone* was playing a trick on him.

Peg decided it was time to tell Patch the true story of Captain Cutthroat's Treasure.

"Captain Cutthroat was the most black-hearted pirate that ever put to sea," whispered Peg. "Before he died, he did a deal with a demon!

"They say the demon still guards the treasure. No one who sets foot on this island ever lives to tell the tale. We should leave."

Now!

But Patch needed that treasure.
He wasn't giving up yet.
At last they found *the spot* and
Patch began to dig.

The Spot!

Peg could hear a noise
like thunder rumbling.
She was afraid it might be
the demon waking up.

Kippers and Codswallop!

Now it seemed to be getting hotter.
The rumbling was coming closer.
Even Patch started looking
over his shoulder.

Suddenly, out of the trees ran
two wild creatures, making
terrible noises!

Peg was sure the demon had sent
the creatures to scare them away.
Pierre and Portside agreed.
Even Patch thought it might be
time to leave!

Creeping Crayfish!

In a blink of Peg's good eye,
The Little Pearl had set sail.
Soon Skeleton Island was just
a dot far behind them.

Patch looked back at those two wild creatures. For a moment, he thought they looked very like his old enemies – Bones and Jones!

Once again, *The Little Pearl* brought Patch and his valiant crew home safely.

She might not be as big and
shiny as Mum and Dad's ship,
but she never let them down.

Patch didn't need treasure. He had his own little ship and his own *capable* crew.

What more could any little pirate want?

★ Pirate Patch ★

ROSE IMPEY   NATHAN REED

All priced at £4.99

Orchard Colour Crunchies are available from all good bookshops,
or can be ordered direct from the publisher:
Orchard Books, PO BOX 29, Douglas IM99 1BQ
Credit card orders please telephone 01624 836000
or fax 01624 837033 or visit our internet site: www.orchardbooks.co.uk
or e-mail: bookshop@enterprise.net for details.

To order please quote title, author and ISBN
and your full name and address.
Cheques and postal orders should be made payable to 'Bookpost plc.'
Postage and packing is FREE within the UK
(overseas customers should add £2.00 per book).

Prices and availability are subject to change.